Annushka's Voyage

by Edith Tarbescu
Illustrated by Lydia Dabcovich

CLARION BOOKS / NEW YORK

Clarion Books
a Houghton Mifflin Company imprint
215 Park Avenue South, New York, NY 10003
Text copyright © 1998 by Edith Tarbescu
Illustrations copyright © 1998 by Lydia Dabcovich
Illustrations executed in pen and ink, acrylic and colored pencils.
Text is 14.5-point Zapf Book Medium.
Printed in Singapore.

Library of Congress Cataloging-in-Publication Data
Tarbescu, Edith.
Annushka's voyage / by Edith Tarbescu ; illustrated by Lydia Dabcovich.
p. cm.
Summary: The Sabbath candlesticks given to them by their grandmother when they leave Russia help
two sisters make it safely to join their father in New York.
ISBN 0-395-64366-X
[1. Emigration and immigration—Fiction. 2. Russian Americans—Fiction. 3. Jews—Fiction.]
I. Dabcovich, Lydia, ill. II. Title.
PZ7.T1653An 1998
[E]—dc20 96-26681
CIP
AC
TWP 10 9 8 7 6 5 4 3 2 1

"Anya," Grandma called. "Hurry! A letter from Papa just arrived."

I jumped up so fast the cow swished her tail in my face.

Papa's letter was filled with funny pictures. There were drawings of the doll factory where he worked and of the pigeons on his roof.

He wrote, "People say the streets here are paved with gold. I am saving money to buy steamship tickets for Anya and Tanya."

That's when Tanya started crying. "First Mama died and went to heaven, then Papa left for America."

I put my arms around her and wiped away her tears. "He'll send for us soon. You'll see."

Early each morning, even before it was light, we worked around the farm. In the afternoons we helped Grandma make puddings and potato pancakes. Before bed we had Hebrew lessons with Grandpa. And we waited.

After more than a year, two steamship tickets came in the mail with a letter from Papa telling us he'd meet us in New York.

"We're going to America! We're going to America!" shouted Tanya, jumping up and down.

I could tell that Grandma was sad, so I hugged her and said, "I'll write every day, and I'll draw funny pictures."

The evening before we left, we had one last Sabbath dinner together. Then Grandma took the Sabbath candlesticks off the table and gave one to me and one to Tanya.

"I hope these will bring you good luck," she said. "They were a wedding present from my mother."

Grandpa gave us going-away presents, too. He gave me a book of Russian fairy tales, and he gave Tanya a doll. Then he bent down and whispered, "Don't forget your homeland, Annushka." Grandpa had always called me by my nickname.

The next morning Grandpa hitched his horse to the wagon, and we drove to the train station. I tried not to cry, but I couldn't help myself. I must have looked as if I'd been peeling a bushel of onions.

The train whistle blew, and Grandpa said, "Take care of Tanya, Annushka. And remember, we love you."

"Hold hands," added Grandma. "And don't talk to strangers."

"Goodbye, Annushka. Goodbye, Tanya. We love you."

I pressed my nose to the window, and the last thing I saw was the red scarf Grandma was waving.

For a while, everything looked the same: the roads, the animals, even the houses.

Everything changed when we got to Holland. There were cobblestone streets and small, brick houses. As soon as we got off the train we were sent to a big building to be examined by doctors. There were so many people speaking so many different languages.

Our ship arrived that evening.

It was gigantic!

I took Tanya's hand and led her up the gangplank. "Don't be afraid," I told Tanya, but my heart was pounding.

When we paused on the deck, men in uniforms shouted, "Keep moving, keep moving."

We kept going down, down, down until we reached the basement of the ship. It was dark and scary, especially with the engines running.

We slept on thin mattresses in small wooden bunks, one on top of the other, like shelves in a closet. There were more than a thousand people huddled together. The air smelled bad because there was nowhere to take a bath. The days were long and there was nowhere to go.

A kind lady took pity on us.
"Come," she said. "And bring your blankets with you."

We followed her out to the third-class deck. "You can't go above," she said, making a face. "That's the rule. But you can come out here any time you want."

It felt good to breathe the salty fresh air. A lanky man with frizzy hair played an accordion, and a short lady sang Hungarian songs.

"Annushka, maybe crossing the ocean won't be so bad after all," Tanya said happily. "Look how blue the sky is. And it goes on forever."

But one afternoon during the second week the sun hid behind the clouds, and the sky turned black. Then the wind started to howl.

"A storm," someone shouted, and everybody ran below.

For days the ship rocked back and forth. I was cold and miserable and so seasick I couldn't move from my bunk, except to go to the bathroom. I heard Tanya calling, but I couldn't help her.

Finally the storm passed and the skies cleared. I walked to the dining room to get food for Tanya and myself. The soup was watery, and the potatoes were cold, but we were so hungry they tasted good. Then I read to Tanya from Grandpa's book. Before Tanya fell asleep I heard her tell her doll, "Don't cry. You'll see Papa soon. I promise. And he'll never leave you again. Never. Ever."

For a whole week we didn't see anything but sea and sky. Then one day we heard someone shout, "I can see land! Come quick!"

When we ran up to the deck, a crowd was already gathered there.

"I see New York Harbor," cried a short, chubby girl.

"I see the Statue of Liberty," shouted a boy. He was small and skinny, and he was carrying a sack almost as big as himself.

Suddenly Tanya asked, "What if Papa doesn't find us?"

"He will," I told her. But I was scared, too. What if he didn't find us? There were so many people on the ship. What would we do then?

As the ship pulled into the harbor, there was so much pushing and jostling, Tanya's hand slipped out of mine, and she disappeared in the crowd.

"Tanya!" I screamed. "Where are you?"

"Over here!" she shouted back. "Over here . . ."

All I could see were long coats. The sound of Tanya's voice got farther and farther away until I couldn't hear her anymore.

Then I remembered Grandma's candlestick. I reached into my sack and pulled it out. Like the Statue of Liberty holding her torch, I raised the candlestick in the air and waved it, back and forth, back and forth.

At last I saw Tanya's candlestick bobbing up and down in the air as she pushed her way through the crowd. I reached out and grabbed her hand. "Hold on to me, Tanya. And don't let go."

Once the ship had docked, the people who were traveling first and second class got off. The rest of us were herded together and put in small boats. Someone said we were going to Ellis Island to be examined by doctors.

"This way, this way," men shouted as they pointed to a long flight of stairs inside the building.

An elderly woman ahead of us in line turned to me and said, "Be careful—even how you walk up the stairs. If the doctors think you're sick, they will send you back. Make sure they don't put a mark on your back with chalk. It's bad."

I held on to Tanya's hand tightly as we climbed the stairs to the Great Hall.

But a woman pushed in between us, screaming at me in a strange language.

"Anya, don't leave me!" Tanya cried. But I couldn't do anything.

"I'll wait for you," I shouted back as more and more people came between us.

Different doctors checked our heads and our ears; someone even pried my eyelids wide open.

A doctor marked an E on the boy in front of me. The boy's mother started screaming, "Help me, help me, somebody."

❦

Five hours later I was through, but Tanya was still moving through the maze. I waited for Tanya and worried. What if the doctor thought she was sick and sent her back?

Then I saw Tanya! I rushed over and took her hand. We were free to go to the first-floor waiting room. It was full of people waiting for their relatives.

"How will we find Papa?" I asked. I had his name and address pinned to my coat. But where was *Houston Street?*

"Wave your candlestick and I'll wave mine," said Tanya. "That's how I found you."

So we did. Back and forth, back and forth until we heard Papa's voice. "Anya! Tanya! I'm here. I'M HERE!"

Papa hugged us and swung us around, crying in Russian and in English, "*Dobro pozhalovat v Ameriku. Dobro pozhalovat v vashu novuyu stranu!* Welcome to America. Welcome to your new home!" He was so happy, he had tears running down his cheeks.

We left Ellis Island and took a ferry to the Battery.
Then we traveled the rest of the way to Papa's
apartment by horse-drawn trolley.

That night, Papa cooked a special dinner to celebrate our arrival. When Papa asked me to say the Sabbath prayer, I put Grandma's candlesticks on the table and lit the candles. Then I said the prayer.

"I'm proud of you," said Papa. "You said the prayer perfectly."

"Thank you," I answered.

Later that night, as Tanya slept next to me, I lay in the dark, listening to the strange new sounds from the street below, and I thought of Grandpa and his special way of saying, "Take care of Tanya, Annushka. And remember, we love you."

The author's mother,
Esther Malasky Roseman (standing), and the
author's aunt, Rose Malasky Levine, after
they arrived in America, circa 1917.
Collection of Edith Tarbescu.

Author's Note

In the late 1800s during the reign of Czar Alexander III the persecution of Jews in Russia worsened. Laws were passed limiting the number of Jewish students admitted to high schools and universities. *Pogroms* or rampages against Jews in various parts of Russia left entire villages burned to the ground. Jews were no longer allowed to own land outside of towns. Overcrowding and poverty increased. As a result, hundreds of thousands of Jews fled to America. Often a whole family would save money to enable one member to make the trip across the Atlantic Ocean to what they called "The Golden Land."

Ever since I was a child I heard the story of how my mother made that journey at the age of thirteen. This is her story.